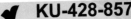

LITTLE LIBRARY

The Three Little Pigs

AND OTHER STORIES

Retold by Margaret Carter
Illustrated by Hilda Offen

Kingfisher Books

Kingfisher Books, Grisewood & Dempsey Ltd,
Elsley House, 24–30 Great Titchfield Street,
London W1P 7AD

First published by Kingfisher Books in 1993
2 4 6 8 10 9 7 5 3 1

BRITISH LIBRARY CATALOGUING IN PUBLICATION DATA
A catalogue record for this book is available from
the British Library
ISBN 1 85697 082 5

Designed by The Pinpoint Design Company
Phototypeset by Waveney Typesetters, Norwich
Printed in Great Britain by
BPCC Paulton Books Limited

Contents

The Three Little Pigs

Traditional English

Three little pigs once set off to seek their fortunes. "Tra, la, la," they sang as they marched down the road.

They hadn't gone far when they met a man with a load of straw. "Could you spare me some straw to build a house?" asked the first pig. "Certainly," said the man. So the pig built himself a house of straw.

Then along came a wolf, a hungry wolf, looking for a pig for his supper.

"Little pig, little pig, may I come in?" he asked, seeing the house of straw.

"Not by the hair on my chinny chin chin," said the little pig.

"Then I'll huff and I'll puff and I'll blow your house down!" snarled the wolf. Which he did, and that was the end of that little pig.

The second little pig had built himself a house of sticks. He settled himself in, very nice and cosy – and along came that wolf, still hungry. "Little pig, little pig, may I come in?" he asked.

"Not by the hair on my chinny chin chin," laughed the second pig.

"Then I'll huff and I'll puff and I'll blow your house down," roared the wolf. And he did.

In went the wolf and that was the end of the second little pig.

Now there was only the third little pig left, but he was the clever

one. He'd built his house of bricks. The old wolf came along and asked if he could come in, but the third little pig laughed and said, "Not by the hair on my chinny chin chin."

"Then I'll huff and I'll puff and I'll blow your house down," growled the wolf. "Blow away, then," said the third little pig.

But however much the wolf puffed and huffed he couldn't blow the house down. Then he noticed that the chimney was quite wide.

He climbed onto the roof and began to slide down the chimney.

But the third little pig was ready for him: under the chimney he put a big bucket of water. Down came the wolf, plop! into the water. And that was the end of him!

So the little pig lived happily in his house of bricks and no one ever troubled him again.

The Travelling Musicians

The Brothers Grimm

There was once a donkey who, old and tired, could no longer work for his living. "My master may not want to keep me," he thought, "now that I cannot work, but my voice is as strong as ever. I'll go to the Town of Bremen and sing for money to buy my food."

On the way he met a dog. "I'm weary," he told the donkey. "I can no longer run fast. I'm no use to anyone."

"But your voice is still splendid," said the donkey. "Come with me to Bremen and we'll earn our living by singing together."

"You're right," said the dog. "I can still bark and howl. Thank you – I'll certainly come with you."

They hadn't gone far when they saw a cat. "What do you think?" she said. "Just because I'm old and can't catch as many mice as I used to, my master has bought a kitten!"

The donkey and the dog told the cat their plan and invited her to join them. "I'd be delighted," said she; "my miaouw is as loud as ever!"

On their way to Bremen they

met a cock. He looked furious. "Do you know what?" he asked them. "The family is planning to cook me and eat me for dinner!" and he gave a very loud cock-a-doodle-doo!

The donkey, the cat and the dog all had the same idea. "Please join us," they said, and "I'll be pleased to," he said.

They journeyed on together...
"I am hungry," said the cat.
"Me too," said the dog.
"And me," said the donkey.
"So am I," said the cock.
Then they saw a cottage.

"Perhaps they will give us food," said the donkey, and they all crept up to the window and looked in. Inside three robbers were counting gold.

"OOH!" brayed the donkey. His voice was so loud that all the robbers ran for the door.

They trod on the cat, who scratched them. They tripped over the dog, who bit them. They bumped into the donkey, who kicked them. "Take that!" screeched the cock and clawed them.

The four friends went into the cottage, had a good meal and made their home there. So they never sang in Bremen, which was just as well because between you and me their voices really were terrible!

Henny Penny

Traditional English

One day Henny Penny was in the farmyard when plop! something fell on her head. "Goodness," she said, "the sky is falling down. I must go and tell the king."

On her way she met Cocky Locky. "I'm going to the palace to tell the king the sky is falling down. Won't you come with me?"

So Cocky Locky came with her and quite soon they met Ducky Lucky. "We're telling the king the sky

is falling down!" they said.

"I'll come too," said Ducky Lucky.

"Me too," said Goosey Loosey.

Round the next corner they met

Turkey Lurkey. "Hurry, hurry, we're off to tell the king the sky is falling down. Will you come too?"

"Yes," he said.

Next they met Foxy Loxy. As soon as they told him where they were going he said he'd join them. But he played a trick on them.

"Allow me to show you a short cut to the palace," he said, and he led them into a deep, dark wood. Then he showed them a deep, dark hole. "In here," he said.

What they didn't know was that inside the hole was Mrs Fox and five hungry fox cubs. In went Turkey Lurkey and snap! he was gone. In went Goosey Loosey – snap! Then

Ducky Lucky – snap! But Cocky Locky made such a noise before they'd snapped him up that Henny Penny took fright and ran.

She ran and ran all the way back to the farmyard and there she stayed. So of course she never did tell the king the sky was falling down.

25

The Dragon and the Monkey

Traditional Chinese

Far away in the China Seas there lived two dragons, husband and wife.

The husband dragon was always anxious to give his wife anything she wanted, so when she said she didn't feel at all well, he was very upset. "Anything I can do?" he asked.

"The only thing I'd like," she said, "is a monkey's heart to eat."

(Not very pleasant, as I think you'll agree).

"There are no monkeys hereabouts," said her husband. "I'll swim off to Africa to find one."

After a great deal of swimming and puffing the dragon came to Africa. "Care for a trip to China?" he asked the first monkey he met.

"Why not?" said the monkey. He climbed onto the dragon's back and off they went. The dragon hadn't

mentioned the monkey's heart, but he brought up the subject when they got to China. The monkey was not keen.

"No way," he thought to himself but he kept his cool and said, "Why ever didn't you tell me before? You see, when I travel I always leave my heart behind. We'll have to go back for it."

Dragon sighed: "Very well!" So, swim swim, puff puff and there at last was Africa. Off jumped the monkey and into the nearest tree. "Sorry, but my heart stays inside me! Thanks for the ride!" he said.

So the dragon's wife never got her monkey's heart after all.

LITTLE LIBRARY

Red Books to collect:

Beauty and the Beast
and Other Stories

▲

Cinderella
and Other Stories

▲

Goldilocks
and Other Stories

▲

Little Red Riding Hood
and Other Stories